The FIREFIGHTERS' THANKSGIVING

by **MARIBETH BOELTS**   illustrated by **TERRY WIDENER**

PUFFIN BOOKS

To all firefighters,
Waterloo Fire Rescue,
Darwin and Mick. —M. B.

For L.S.W. (25) —T. W.

PUFFIN BOOKS
Published by the Penguin Group
Penguin Young Readers Group, 345 Hudson Street,
New York, New York 10014, U.S.A.
Penguin Group (Canada), 90 Eglinton Avenue East, Suite 700,
Toronto, Ontario, Canada M4P 2Y3
(a division of Pearson Penguin Canada Inc.)
Penguin Books Ltd, 80 Strand, London WC2R 0RL, England
Penguin Ireland, 25 St Stephen's Green, Dublin 2, Ireland
(a division of Penguin Books Ltd)
Penguin Group (Australia), 250 Camberwell Road, Camberwell, Victoria 3124,
Australia (a division of Pearson Australia Group Pty Ltd)
Penguin Books India Pvt Ltd, 11 Community Centre, Panchsheel Park,
New Delhi - 110 017, India
Penguin Group (NZ), Cnr Airborne and Rosedale Roads, Albany, Auckland 1310,
New Zealand (a division of Pearson New Zealand Ltd)
Penguin Books (South Africa) (Pty) Ltd, 24 Sturdee Avenue,
Rosebank, Johannesburg 2196, South Africa

Registered Offices: Penguin Books Ltd, 80 Strand,
London WC2R 0RL, England

First published in the United States of America by
G. P. Putnam's Sons, a division of Penguin Young Readers Group, 2004
Published by Puffin Books,
a division of Penguin Young Readers Group, 2006

10 9 8 7 6 5 4 3 2

Text copyright © Maribeth Boelts, 2004
Illustrations copyright © Terry Widener, 2004
All rights reserved

THE LIBRARY OF CONGRESS HAS CATALOGED THE G. P. PUTNAM'S SONS EDITION AS FOLLOWS:
Boelts, Maribeth.
The firefighters' Thanksgiving / by Maribeth Boelts; illustrated by Terry Widener.
p.   cm.
Summary: Calls to fires, an injured friend, and cooking disasters threaten
to keep a group of firefighters from enjoying Thanksgiving dinner.
ISBN: 0-399-23600-7 (hc)
[1. Fire fighters—Fiction. 2. Thanksgiving Day—Fiction. 3. Stories in rhyme.]
I. Widener, Terry, ill. II. Title.
PZ8.3.B599545 Fi 2004 [E]—dc21 00-045909

Puffin Books ISBN 0-14-240631-7

Designed by Gunta Alexander
Text set in Sodium
The art was done in Golden acrylics on Strathmore paper

Manufactured in China

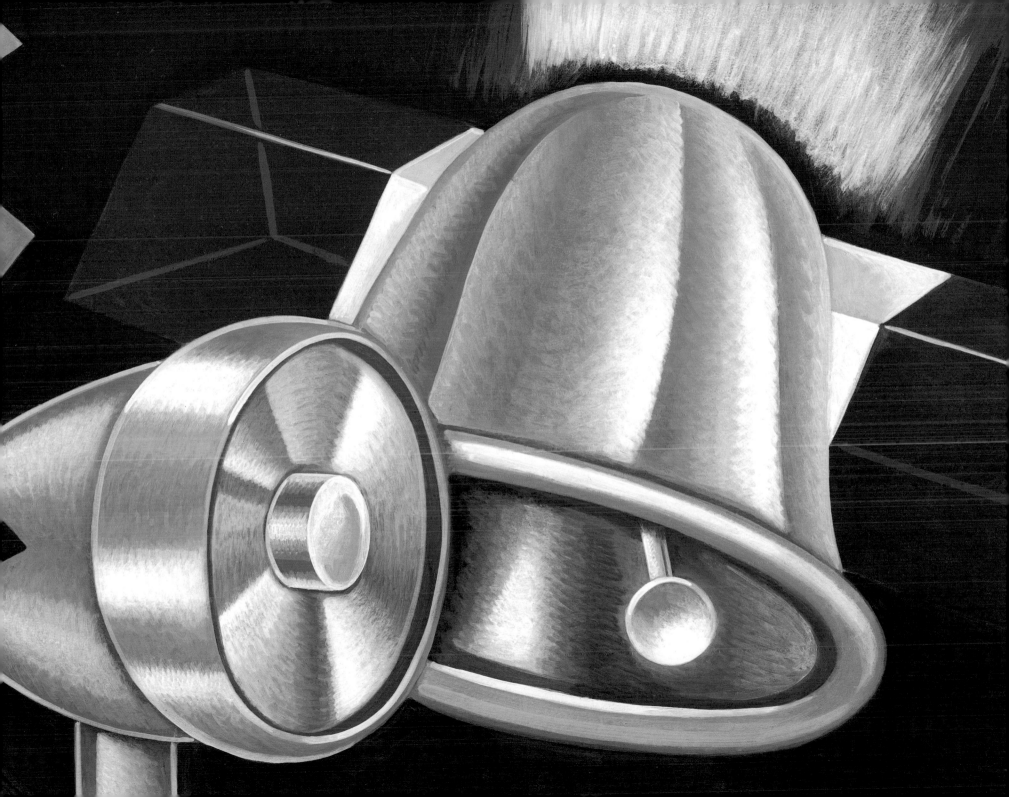

Thanksgiving Day—this shift's begun.
Ten firefighters at Station 1.

Lou says, "I can cook today."
A list is made. They're on their way.

A turkey, pumpkin, yeast, potatoes,
ice cream, yams and ripe tomatoes.
The cart is full, the shopping's through.

A call comes in—it's 9:02.

Sooty, smoky, back to the store.

They help mop ice cream from the floor.

They split the tab, then peel and clean.

A call comes in—it's 12:15.

They wash the trucks, hang hose to dry.

Roll out crust for pumpkin pie.

Pack up gear and fill the tank.

Plan the next big rookie prank.

The turkey's frozen. Is it too late?

A call comes in—it's 2:08.

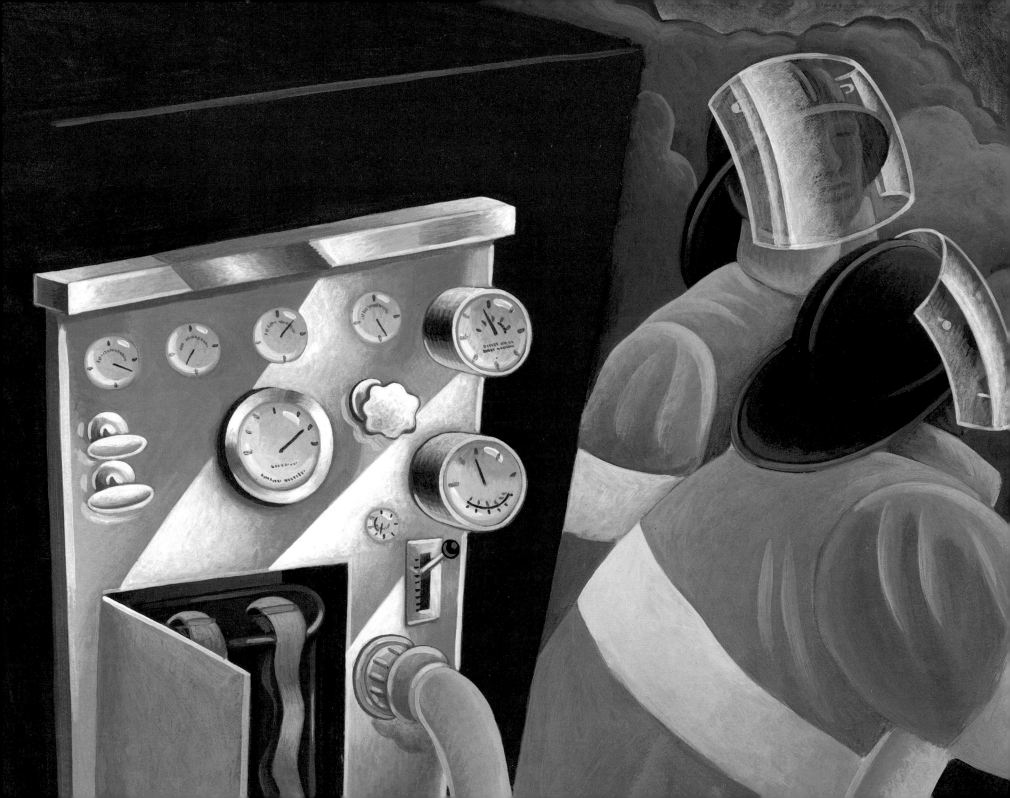

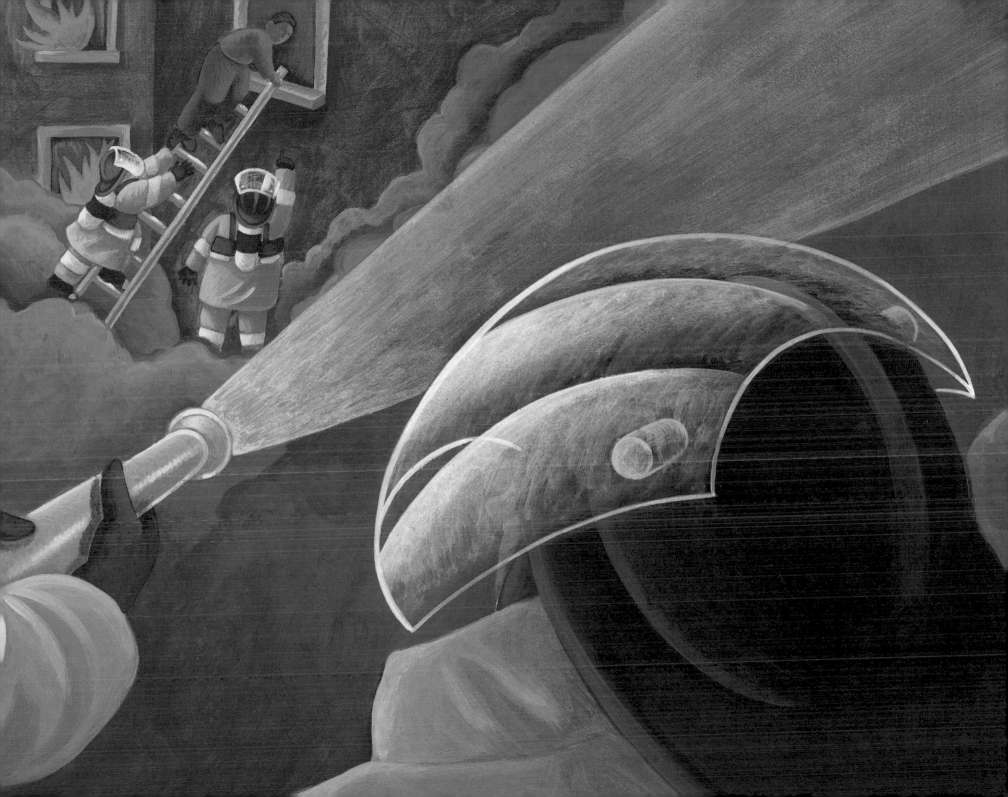

They check equipment, fix a tire.

Record the details of the fire.

Put potatoes on to boil.

Refuel the trucks and change the oil.

Throw out pie crust, start again.

A call comes in—it's 4:10.

Lou is hurt! Firefighters worry.

To the hospital in a hurry.

The meal forgotten, some pace, some pray.

They get the news . . .

Back at the station, night is falling.

Families will soon be calling.

The turkey's raw, the potatoes, too.

No pies, no bread, just thoughts of Lou.

They wash the trucks and hose the floor.

A call comes in—it's 8:04.

While they fight fires,
a feast is spread—
Turkey, stuffing, pies and bread.
A note is on the table, too:

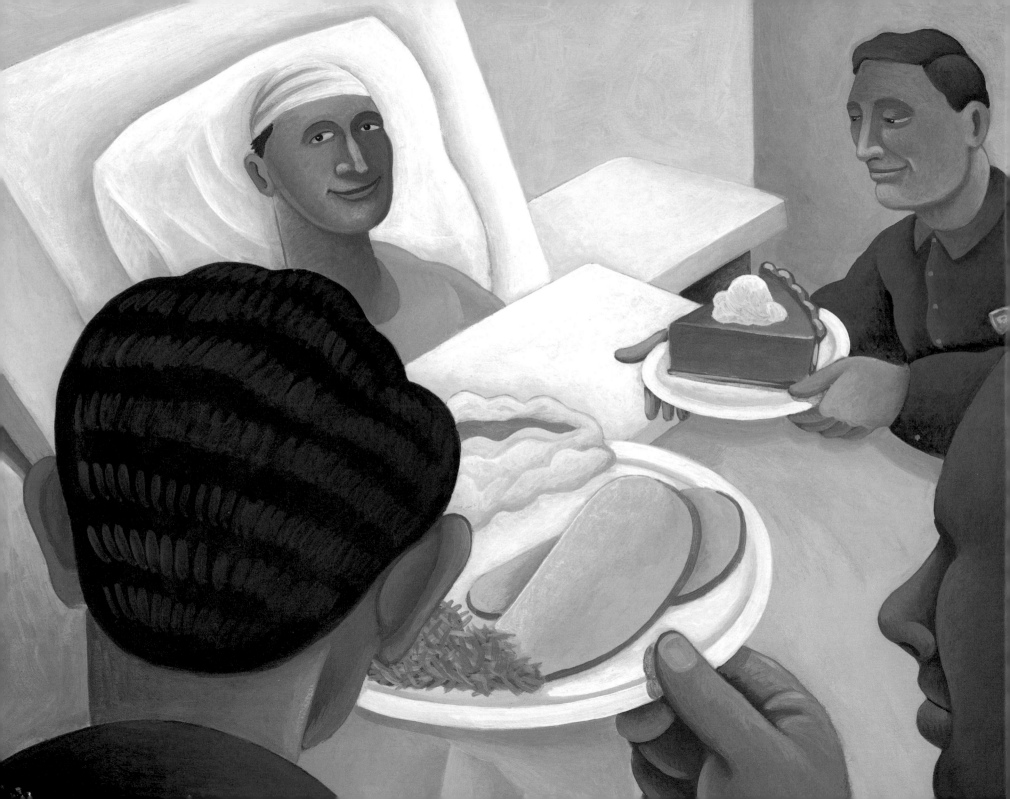